For the little Soissonais –
Thibaud, Priscille, Albert,
Adrion, Jean and Solène – a
story from deep in the forest.
OL

Little Mole,
Please Open the Door!

By Orianne Lallemand
Illustrations by Claire Frossard

AUZOU

BRRRRR! *What a cold, winter night,* thought Little Mole, snuggling into her warm bed.

KNOCK KNOCK KNOCK!

Who's that knocking at the door?

It's Frog, and he's freezing!

Mole had just settled Frog on the sofa when . . .

KNOCK KNOCK KNOCK!

Now, who's at the door?

It's Squirrel, shivering in the snow!

Squirrel had just nestled in next to Frog when . . .

KNOCK KNOCK KNOCK!

Who can that be at the door?

It's poor Badger, soaked to the skin.

Badger had just crawled under the blanket next to Squirrel when . . .

KNOCK KNOCK KNOCK!

Who is at the door?

15

It's Mama Chickadee and her babies.
"It's much too cold in our nest tonight," said Mama.

Mole had just tucked the Chickadee family into her spare bed when . . . KNOCK KNOCK KNOCK!

Who's that banging on the door?

"I'm going to eat you all!" growls Wolf.

"Quick!" Badger yells. "Attack!"

BANG! BOOM! OUCH!

Badger and Squirrel begin hitting Wolf with a pair of pots while Mama Chickadee and Frog tie him up!

BAA-DA-BOOM!

Wolf falls to the floor.
Mama and Frog have him restrained in a flash.

25

The animals are hungry after all the excitement, so Mole prepares a big pot of her special soup.

When . . .

KNOCK KNOCK KNOCK!

Who could possibly be at the door now?

27

Why it's Hedgehog, Owl, Mouse, and Rabbit.
They want to get warm too.

MMMM! Warm and dry at last, they all enjoy a delicious bowl of soup . . .

Even Wolf!

Publisher: Gauthier Auzou
Editorial director: Florence Pierron
Designer: Annaïs Tassone, Alice Vignaux
Production Management: Jean-Christophe Collett
Production: Salima Hragui
Project Management for the English Edition: Ariane Laine-Forrest
English Translation: MaryChris Bradley

ISBN: 978-2-7338-6146-2

First published in France as *Petite taupe ouvre-moi ta porte !*
Copyright © 2011 Editions AUZOU
24-32 rue des Amandiers 75020 Paris, France

Printed in China.

 www.auzou-us.com